KU-167-685

for Kate Colquhoun

... who went voling   M.W.

for Gregory   B.F.

First published 1992
by Walker Books Ltd
87 Vauxhall Walk
London SE11 5HJ

Text © 1992 Martin Waddell
Illustrations © 1992 Barbara Firth

The right of Martin Waddell to be
identified as the author of this work
has been asserted by him in accordance
with the Copyright, Designs and
Patents Act, 1988.

Printed and bound in
Hong Kong by Dai Nippon
Printing Co. Ltd

British Library Cataloguing
in Publication Data
A catalogue record for this book
is available from the British Library.

ISBN 0-7445-2180-7

Sam Vole
and his
Brothers

written by

Martin Waddell

illustrated by

Barbara Firth

HIGHLAND LIBRARIES
REGIONAL LIBRARY
92 04052
WITHDRAWN

WALKER BOOKS
LONDON

Sam Vole had big brothers,
Arthur and Henry.
Sam wanted to do things
all by himself, but wherever
he went his brothers went too.

"I'm going voling for nuts,"
Sam told Mother. "I'm going
voling all by myself."

Sam went voling out in the garden,
but Arthur and Henry went too.
They brought home more nuts than Sam,
enough for them all.
Sam gave his nuts to Mother.

"I'm going voling for grass,"
Sam told Mother.
"I'm going voling all by myself."
Sam went voling out in the garden,
but Arthur and Henry went too.
They carried home more grass than Sam,
enough for them all.
Sam gave his grass to Mother.

"I'm going voling for daisies,"
Sam told Mother.
"I'm going voling all by myself."
Sam went voling out in the garden,
but Arthur and Henry went too.
 They picked more daisies than Sam,
  enough for them all.
   Sam gave his daisies to Mother.

When they all went to bed
Sam could not sleep.
He lay awake thinking;
I want to do something all by myself.

Early next morning he did it.
He slipped out of the house
and into the garden
and he went voling
alone.

He voled and he voled
all by himself
and he sang and he danced,
for he liked it so much
without brothers.

He voled and he voled
all by himself
and he ran and he jumped,
for he liked it a lot
without brothers.

He voled and he voled
all by himself
and he walked and he whistled,
for he still liked it a bit
without brothers.

He voled and he voled
all by himself.
Then he stopped and he stood
and he listened.
He didn't like it at all
without brothers.

Sam sat and felt sad
without brothers.

Then he saw …

Arthur and Henry,
his brothers.

And Sam said,
"I've been voling alone
all by myself
now I'll vole with you,
you're my brothers."

And they voled round
the garden together.

And then …

the brothers voled happily home.